NADINE
DREAMS OF
HOME

Bernard Ashley

NADINE DREAMS OF HOME

With illustrations by
Ollie Cuthbertson

Barrington Stoke

First published in 2014 in Great Britain by
Barrington Stoke Ltd
18 Walker Street, Edinburgh, EH3 7LP

www.barringtonstoke.co.uk

Reprinted 2016

This story was first published in a different form in
Stacks of Stories (Hodder Children's Books, 1997)

Text © 2014 Bernard Ashley
Illustrations © 2014 Ollie Cuthbertson

A CIP catalogue record for this book is available
from the British Library upon request

ISBN: 978-1-78112-369-0

Printed in China by Leo

Contents

1   Not a Word   1

2   Like a Book   5

3   At the Library   9

4   A Picture of Home   13

5   This Is Now   25

6   Deep in Her Bones   31

7   Thump, Thump, Thump   37

8   Together   45

Chapter 1
Not a Word

Nadine looked round the big classroom. It had more than 30 children in it, but there were no other Goma children. No one else who spoke Nadine's language.

It was real scary, here in Britain. Not scary like when you had to run away from the stink of burning buildings or the sound of shooting. And not scary like when you had to try to hide from the rebel soldiers with your mother and your little brother. But scary in other ways.

There was the noise of London – that was scary. The lorries rattled like troop carriers, and the buses hissed their brakes like rockets skimming across the sky. And when the low planes came into City Airport – Nadine's mother still ducked her head as if they might be about to drop bombs.

And there was another sort of scary, which was just as bad, in its own way. The scary of being on their own, the three of them, in the flats where they lived, as high as kites fly. The three of them without Nadine's father, Fabrice. He had got them out of Goma on the last plane before the rebels took over the airstrip and took Fabrice off with them.

So Nadine, her mother and Prince were on their own without a word of English. Nadine's father had been a teacher, and he spoke good French and English. If only he were here, he would help them in this foreign land.

Nadine came to school every day and tried like mad to understand what people were saying. And sometimes she could pick out a few words. But at night she cried for her father and went to sleep with her face stained with tears.

She dreamed one special dream – that one day she would go to the airport with her mother and brother, and see her father coming through that Arrivals door. Coming to live with them, to make them all together again. After that, everything would be a million times better.

Chapter 2
Like a Book

Nadine's teacher, who was a kind man, clapped his hands. Nadine sat up straight, on the instant. The teacher clapped his hands again, and one by one the other children stopped what they were doing and listened to him.

His mouth moved and sounds came out. Nadine knew he was speaking to the class, but the words he said meant nothing to Nadine. He looked at her and opened and closed his hands like he was opening and closing a book. He said some more words to her in English.

Nadine thought she understood. The words had something to do with books. But that something wasn't going to happen in here, because now all the other children scraped back their chairs and got books out of trays under their tables and lined up with them at the classroom door. The class was going somewhere else.

Nadine looked in her own tray for a book and took out the only one she had. It was a Maths book.

Eva, who sat on the same table, shook her head and shouted at Nadine, as if she were a bit stupid. Eva took the book off her and put it back in the tray. She jerked her head and made a "come with me" sign with her fingers. She said the same words again to Nadine, but this time she didn't shout.

Those words had to mean "Come with me", or something like that.

And so Nadine went with Eva. She put herself on the end of the line of children at the door. All of them had books in their hands, except her.

Chapter 3
At the Library

This school was not a bit like Nadine's old school in Goma. That had been a church school. It was long and low and painted with a smooth white wash – until the rebels came and the flames blackened it. This English school was made from lots of red bricks laid in patterns. From the yard outside, it seemed to go up high enough to scrape the bellies of the planes as they flew over. Nadine had noticed how much of London went up instead of along.

This school had three floors, with lots of little landings and rooms in between. The library was on the floor below the classroom.

There was a big city library back in Goma, but there wasn't one in Nadine's old school. There, the teacher gave out books from the front of the class.

Nadine's class led her on down the stairs, round and round. Everyone talked, some jumped, until all of a sudden the teacher stopped them.

He looked at the class and spoke in his usual fast way – lots of words that Nadine didn't know. But then, at the end, one word that she did know – "Books".

Nadine smiled. "Books," she said to Eva.

But then the teacher spoke straight at her and pointed back up the stairs. He wagged his finger at Nadine and frowned. Nadine knew what that meant, no problem. That look needed no words, in any language. He wasn't pleased. She had spoken when he wanted silence.

Nadine's face went long and her mouth went small. It was the first time her teacher had been upset with her.

Chapter 4
A Picture of Home

The children went into the library. There were lots and lots of books, but the library didn't just have books. All down one side of the room there was a line of tables with computers on them.

The teacher sat at a table and talked to the children about the books they had chosen. Some kept the ones they had. Others went off to choose something different, in between laughing and pulling faces through the shelves.

Then the teacher clapped his hands again, loud as a gunshot, and shouted at them, fierce like a soldier.

The teacher stood up and pointed at three children. Then he shouted some more fast, angry words. The three children went and stood by the door, hanging their heads – but Nadine could see they were smiling at the floor.

But Nadine wasn't smiling. No way! She had shivered at the anger in the teacher's soldier-voice, and then all at once she was crying.

The shouting had been just like the day before her father had got the family away from Goma. That day, the rebel soldiers had lined the teachers up in the school yard like bad children, and then the soldiers had shouted, "You, you and you!" And Nadine always

thanked God that her father hadn't been one of them. Because the three they chose had been marched off round a corner, and the soldiers had fired their guns, three times.

"Nadine." The teacher had come over and now he was offering Nadine a hankie from the box on the table. He bent to her, put his hands together as if in prayer, asking her to forgive him. "Come with me. Come on," he said.

Nadine went with him. Even through her tears she understood those words. But she knew she couldn't even start to make the teacher understand what had made her cry. Perhaps one day she would, when her English was better. If she could ever bear to tell him. If she could bear to think how much danger her father was still in, captured by those rebels and taken off to another place.

The teacher led Nadine to a computer and switched it on. "Eva, come," he said.

Eva came over. She was smiling, one of those double sorts of smiles. She was smiling both because the teacher had picked her to help, and a little bit because she could show off at being good on the computer.

Nadine looked at her. Eva was staring at the screen without blinking. She wasn't saying anything with her mouth, but her face was saying she was going to surprise Nadine with something. She had the cool look of Nadine's father when he did one of his birthday party tricks.

And all of a sudden Eva turned to Nadine as if she had invented pumpkins. Nadine looked at the computer screen.

In front of Nadine was a page of unreadable writing, but what grabbed her eye was a picture. A picture she knew.

A picture from Goma! There was no mistaking it – a scene of banana trees by Lake Kivu and, in the background, the great Cow Herd mountain. Above the mountain, the sky was clear and blue, with no shell-burst clouds or rocket trails. Nadine could almost hear the lap of the water on the lake-side.

Nadine's mouth opened, and a Bantu sound clicked in her throat. Her eyes closed in a "thank you", and she gave a small smile of great pleasure.

This picture was of her homeland. This was what it was like, outside the town, where there were fish to catch and their family had picnics.

Nadine sat, and she stared. Eva reached for the mouse to change the screen, perhaps to show her another picture, but Nadine stopped her with a word she found she knew.

"No."

From a line of smaller photos down the side of the screen, Nadine could see that there were many more pictures of home, but this one was special. It reminded her of the happiest of times.

The picture stayed. It didn't move or change, but when Nadine half closed her eyes, it seemed to come to life. She could almost see her father walking under those banana trees, swinging a bucket to get water from the lake – and laughing the way he did when things were just as they ought to be.

The teacher had come up behind her and was looking at the picture, too. He was asking her a question, Nadine could tell that. He peered at the text and ran his finger along the line of banana trees on the screen.

"Bananas," he said.

"Bananas," Nadine said too, but her word was more like "ban-an-as".

"Trees," the teacher said.

"Treeees." Now Nadine knew that word, too.

And Nadine's smile told the teacher she had what she wanted. A picture of home.

That night, in the high flat, Nadine had a new dream. It wasn't of her father at the airport, but of her father in the photo on the screen, walking down through the banana trees. But before he got close enough for Nadine to hear his laugh or to touch his hand, he disappeared.

Nadine woke and turned her pillow to the cool side. Then, without waking her mother, she got up and went to the bedroom window.

It was always the same in London. Day or night, it was bright. As she looked out, Nadine could see the River Thames and the tall buildings alongside it. The city. Their new home, because there was no way to go back to Goma until all the fighting had stopped.

And yet it was not their true home, because there was something missing.

Chapter 5
This Is Now

It was a week before Library Time again. And in that week, Nadine learned lots of new words in English.

Now she could say "me" and "you" and "please" and "thanks" and "sick". And now she went to one of the little rooms on a turn of the staircase for special lessons in English with Mrs Hussein, who came in just for Nadine.

Nadine found that the muscles she had to use to make English words worked all right, but she never used the muscles which make smiles.

Until they went to choose books again. Nadine had chosen a picture book without words. But then she put it back – and she went direct to a computer and sat down.

Mr Cooper, the teacher – now she could say his name – came over. He spoke to her, and Nadine knew some of the words he said. "I know …" he said, and "You like …" Then he asked Eva to join them again. Eva turned the computer on and Nadine used the mouse to call up the page she wanted.

The page about Goma with its picture of home.

All over again, Eva and the rest of the world disappeared for Nadine. The sounds of the children in the library were stilled and the movements around her were frozen. It was as if she were inside the picture, with the lake and the banana trees. She heard the lapping water and listened hard in case she might be mistaken and it was the sound of her father laughing.

And tears ran down to salt her smile.

When Nadine looked round to see if the other children had seen the tears, they'd all gone. The library was empty, with just the hum of the computer for company. Mr Cooper had led them out, and left Nadine to enjoy her picture of home. Nadine stayed there until she heard the sounds of the others out at play, when she went to catch up with them.

That night, Nadine told her mother about the photo on the screen. Her mother was getting the meal, and either she didn't want to make much of it, or she was too busy.

"That was then," her mother said. "This is now."

And that made Nadine go further. "I sometimes dream that Dad is in the picture," she said.

"That is stupid!" her mother said. "Dad was. We three are what there is now." And she pounded her spices as if they were an enemy. As if they were the rebels back home in Goma.

Then it was the weekend. Nadine's mother spent Saturday showing her which bus took them to the street market, and how to go to the post office to get money. It was as if she was poking Nadine in the ribs with what she was trying to get her to understand.

And on the way home Nadine's mother said, "Forget Dad," in the same matter-of-fact voice she had used to buy the bus tickets.

Chapter 6
Deep in Her Bones

Fridays became very special days for Nadine. In spite of what her mother said, she still couldn't think of London as her home. And on Fridays she got to go to the library to call up her special picture of home on the computer.

Nadine started to learn some of the words on the screen, the way they were written. She could see the words for "banana" and "tree" – while "Goma" looked much the same.

But on one of the days, in Library Time, Ollie Wilson came over and pushed her off the computer. "What's all this?" he wanted to know. "Stupid trees!"

Nadine stared at his thin, white, screwed up face.

"You live in London now!" Ollie said. And he grabbed the mouse, and Nadine's arm, and forced her to stand and watch while he called up pictures of the Olympic stadium, and a Big Wheel, and a famous London clock.

"That's what you want to look at!" he said. "Forget your Africa!"

But most library days the others left Nadine on her own with her picture. She'd look into it with eyes full of longing – but the image of her father laughing under banana trees grew weaker and weaker, Friday by Friday. And even the water in the lake seemed to stop lapping.

One night, on their old TV set, Nadine heard the news reader say "Goma". She couldn't follow all the words, but she sat with her mother and watched. They were both as stiff as bouma trees as they saw pictures of the fighting there. They watched those trucks packed with rebel soldiers, firing into the air and smiling with big eyes at the camera.

It seemed as if the rebels had won another battle.

Nadine didn't sleep that night. But she didn't cry either, because her eyes couldn't make any more tears. Her fear for her father had gone past all that, deep into her bones.

The next day, the minute Nadine was back in school, she asked to go to the library. Mr Cooper let her. He must have seen the news as well. There was another class having Library Time, but there was a spare computer that Nadine was allowed to use.

Nadine called up her picture. She sat there and looked at the image of her homeland until it went into a blur, and then disappeared, as she closed her eyes in a sort of prayer.

Chapter 7
Thump, Thump, Thump

That night, there was a lot of shouting and wailing round the flats, with kids rocking the cars to set off their alarms. They ran away when the blue flashing light of a police car came along. But up on the 7th floor, Nadine and her mother double-locked the door, and pushed a table against it. Who knew where those kids might have run?

And Nadine went cold in her bed when there was a sudden banging on their own door.

She went under the covers, and under
the pillows. So did her mother, with Nadine's

brother, Prince. If they ignored the banging it would go away. The kids outside would move on to hound someone else.

But bang, bang, bang it went.

The banging became a thumping – not knuckles now, but fists. And it was creepy, because there was no calling or shouting. Just thump, thump, thump.

"Come and see what's out here!" the noise seemed to torment.

It was like the rebels who'd come in the night, with guns and petrol.

Nadine and her mother tried to pretend it wasn't happening. But when Prince woke up and started to shout in fear, they had to do something about it.

There had been a pause when they'd thought it had gone away, but then it came again. Thump, thump, thump. These people knew how to bully, like Ollie at school.

Nadine's mother crept from the bedroom and found a long broom. Then she carried Prince to the furthest corner of the kitchen and put him down behind a cupboard, while Nadine picked up a long vegetable knife. And then

Nadine's mother stood back, trembling with every new thump, and Nadine crawled across the table to the little spy hole in the door.

She peered out, ready to see the faces of hate on the other side.

And saw her father standing there.

Her father!

Thin, tired, beard all scrawny and grey, his body lost in a big English coat – but it was her father! With those father's eyes that never change.

"Dad!" Nadine shouted. "Dad!"

Nadine and her mother pulled against each other in their fever to get the door open. It thudded on Nadine's foot, but she felt no pain.

They dragged her father in and hugged and hugged and hugged him.

And, in between being kissed and fed, Nadine's father told them how badly things had gone for him. He had been taken hostage by the rebels, but he had escaped back across the border and got on a refugee flight to Britain.

And then, after he got to Britain, Nadine's father had spent a week tracking them down.

"So," her father said, looking round, "this is where we are ..."

Chapter 8
Together

The next day, Nadine didn't go to school. She didn't dare go, in case her father wasn't there when she went home. In case it had all been a dream. She stayed with him in the flat, and when he woke up, she told him all the English words she had learned – and he was pleased with her.

But Nadine went to school on the Friday. When it was Library Time, she asked Mr Cooper, as usual, "Please can I use the computer?"

He nodded and spoke some words she didn't understand. Then he said, "Do you want your picture of Goma?"

But Nadine shook her head. "No," she said. "I want to look at a picture of London."

Mr Cooper frowned, and Nadine smiled in reply. A big smile.

"Where I live now," she said. "With my father again, in our new home."

Our books are tested
for children and young people by
children and young people.

Thanks to everyone who consulted on
a manuscript for their time and effort in
helping us to make our books better
for our readers.

More *4u2read* titles ...

All Sorts to Make a World
JOHN AGARD

Shona's day has been packed with characters. First there was 3.2-million-year-old Lucy in the Natural History Museum, and then Pinstripe Man, Kindle Woman, Doctor Bananas and the iPod Twins.

Now Shona and her dad are on a Tube train that's stuck in a tunnel and everyone around them is going ... bananas!

Deadly Letter
MARY HOFFMAN

"Ip dip sky blue. Who's it? Not you."

Prity wants to play with the other children at school, but it's hard when you're the new girl and you don't know the rules. And it doesn't help when you're saddled with a name that sounds like a joke. Will Prity ever fit in?

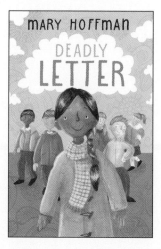

Mozart's Banana
GILLIAN CROSS

Mozart's Banana – a crazy name for a crazy horse. No one can tame Mozart's Banana. Even Sammy Foster failed, and he reckons he's the boss of the school. But then Alice Brett turns up. Alice is as cool as a choc-ice, and she isn't going to let anyone get the better of her, horse or boy ...

Gnomes, Gnomes, Gnomes
ANNE FINE

Sam's a bit obsessed. Any time he gets his hands on some clay, he makes gnomes. Dozens of them live out in the shed. But when Sam's mum needs that space, she says the gnomes will have to go. And so Sam plans a send-off for his little clay friends – a send-off that turns into a night the family will never forget!

More **4u2read** titles ...

Who's a Big Bully Then?
MICHAEL MORPURGO

Olly is a bull. A very big bull.

Darren Bishop is a bully. A very nasty bully.

What happens when one of Darren's victims dares him to take on Olly?

Hostage
MALORIE BLACKMAN

"I'll make sure your dad never sees you again!"

Blindfolded. Alone. Angela has no idea where she is or what will happen next. The only thing she knows is she's been kidnapped. Is she brave enough to escape?

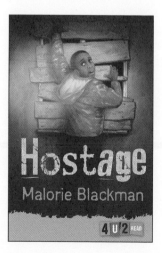

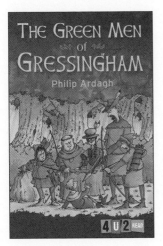

The Green Men of Gressingham

PHILIP ARDAGH

The Green Men are outlaws, living in a forest. Now they have taken Tom prisoner!

What do they want from him?

Who is their secret leader, Robyn-in-the-Hat?

And whose side should Tom be on?

The Red Dragons of Gressingham

PHILIP ARDAGH

The Green Men used to be outlaws. They lived in the forest and did brave deeds.

Now the Green Men are inlaws. They live in the forest and do ... not very much.

The Green men are bored. They need some fun. They need a quest ...

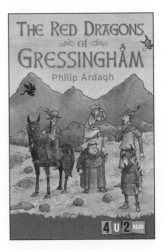

www.barringtonstoke.co.uk

More *Barrington Stoke* titles ...

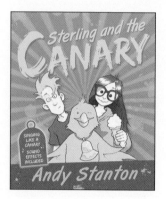

Sterling and the Canary

ANDY STANTON

Lizzie Harris has hair the colour of magic and arms as wonderful as rainbows.

Only thing is, Lizzie Harris won't go out with Sterling Thaxton. Sterling needs help, but who can he ask? Perhaps a canary would do the trick.

Yes, you did read that right. A canary. A very special canary ...

The Story of Matthew Buzzington

ANDY STANTON

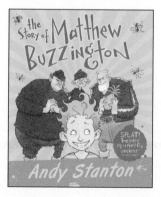

Welcome to the story of Matthew Buzzington. "Who is Matthew Buzzington?" I hear you ask! Well, he's just a normal 10-year-old boy. But Matthew Buzzington can turn into a fly. Imagine that!

It's just, well, he hasn't yet. But with robbers and flying pineapples out to get him he needs to make his super power work! Can he do it?

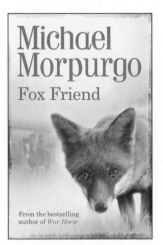

Fox Friend
MICHAEL MORPURGO

When Clare finds a fox cub that has got away from the hunt, she wants to keep him and make him well again. But Clare's dad says foxes are bad. How can Clare keep the cub safe?

The Haunting of Uncle Ron
ANNE FINE

Ian's not keen on Uncle Ron, the world's most boring visitor. Even the voices Uncle Ron hears from the 'Other Side' have nothing interesting to say. Ian can't stand it a moment longer. He must get rid of Uncle Ron. What he needs is a plan – and perhaps a helper ...

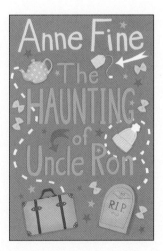

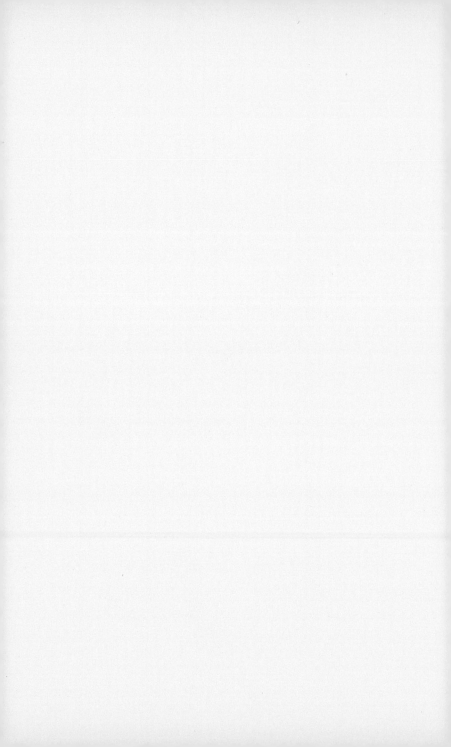